Sing a Song of Circus

Ward Schumaker

Harcourt Brace & Company
San Diego   New York   London

Requests for permission to make copies of any part of the work
should be mailed to: Permissions Department, Harcourt Brace & Company,
6277 Sea Harbor Drive, Orlando, Florida 32887-6777.

Library of Congress Cataloging-in-Publication Data
Schumaker, Ward.
Sing a song of circus/Ward Schumaker.
p.   cm.
Summary: Two balloons escape from their bunch and join the circus,
bringing water to the elephants, serving popcorn and soft drinks,
and playing with the seals.
ISBN 0-15-201363-6
[1. Circus—Fiction. 2. Balloons—Fiction.]
I. Title. PZ7.S3925Si   1997
[E]—dc20   95-47124

First edition
A C E F D B

Printed in Singapore

The illustrations in this book are seven-color hand-separated black-ink drawings.
The display type and text type were set in Officina Sans Book by
Harcourt Brace & Company Photocomposition Center, San Diego, California.
Color separations by United Graphic, Singapore
Printed and bound by Tien Wah Press, Singapore
This book was printed on Cougar Opaque wood-free paper.
Production supervision by Stanley Redfern and Pascha Gerlinger
Designed by Ward Schumaker and Lori McThomas Buley

Special thanks, again, to
Diane D'Andrade and Marcia Wernick

For my brothers
(who form a three-ring circus
all by themselves)
and Matthew

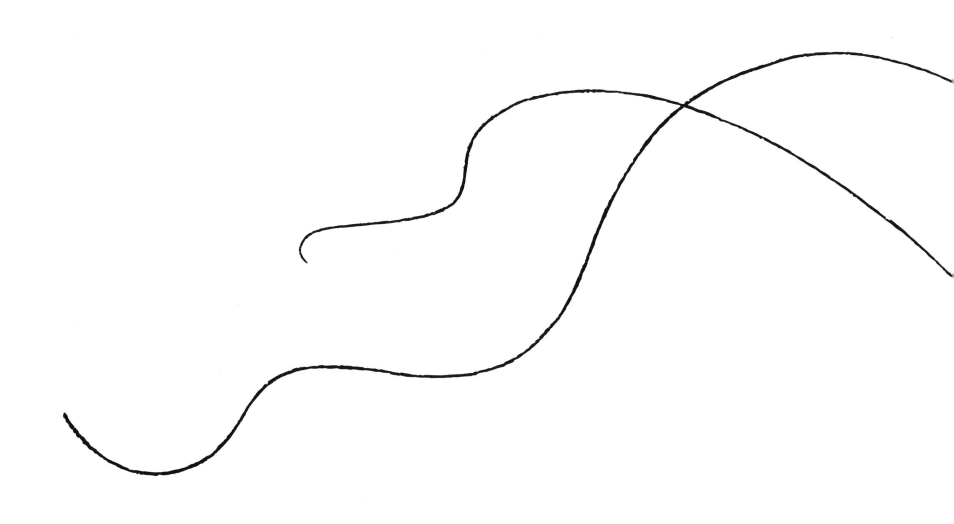

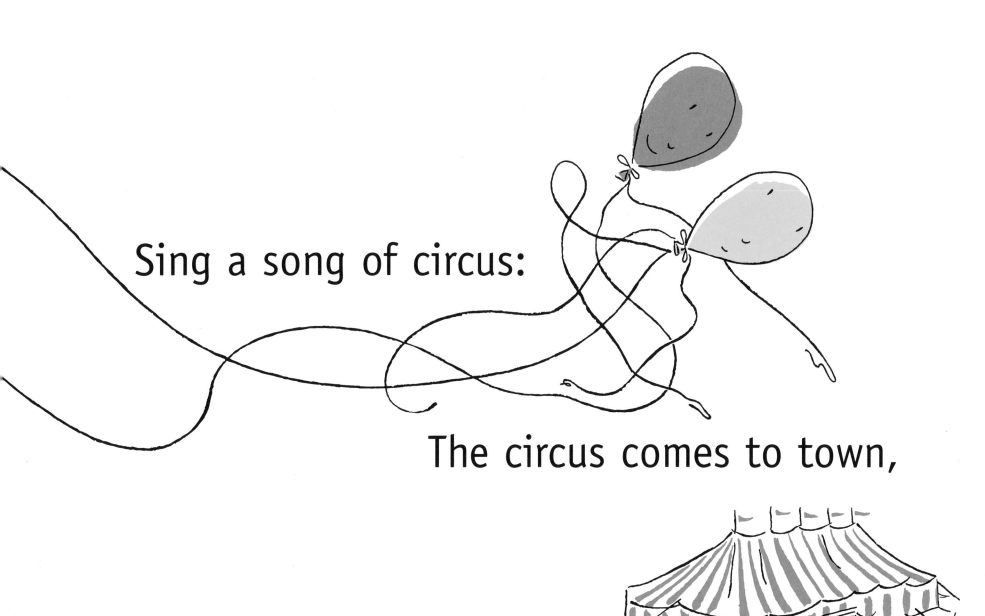

Sing a song of circus:

The circus comes to town,

And in it work ten elephants,

Six lions, and a clown;

A trapeze star, a hairy ape,

Four seals—a kangaroo!

A little duck, a dancing pig—

And why not me and you?

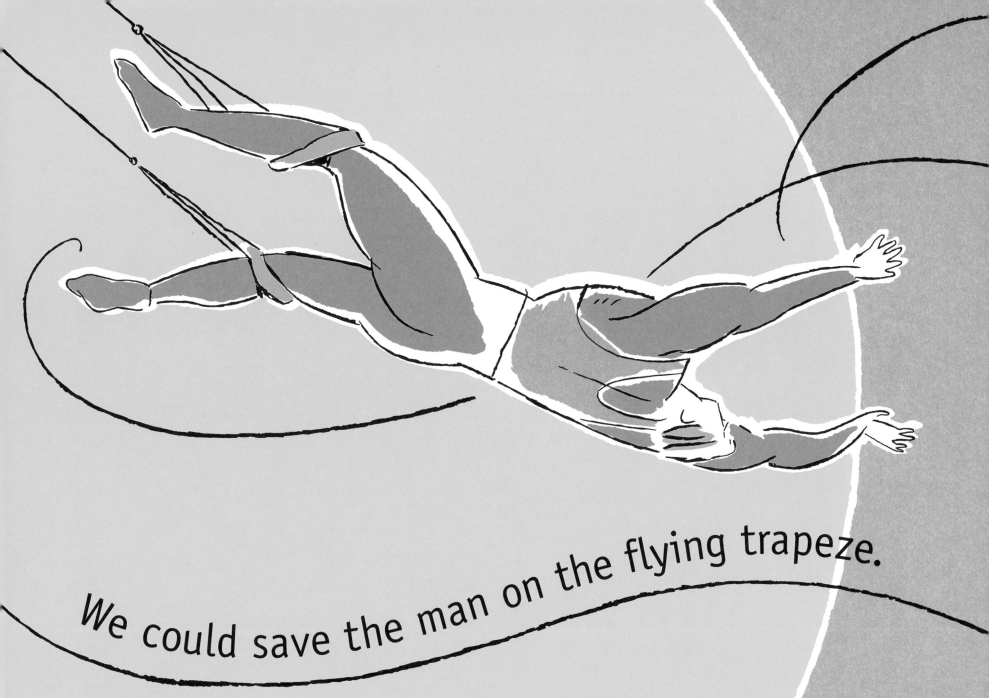

We could save the man on the the flying trapeze.

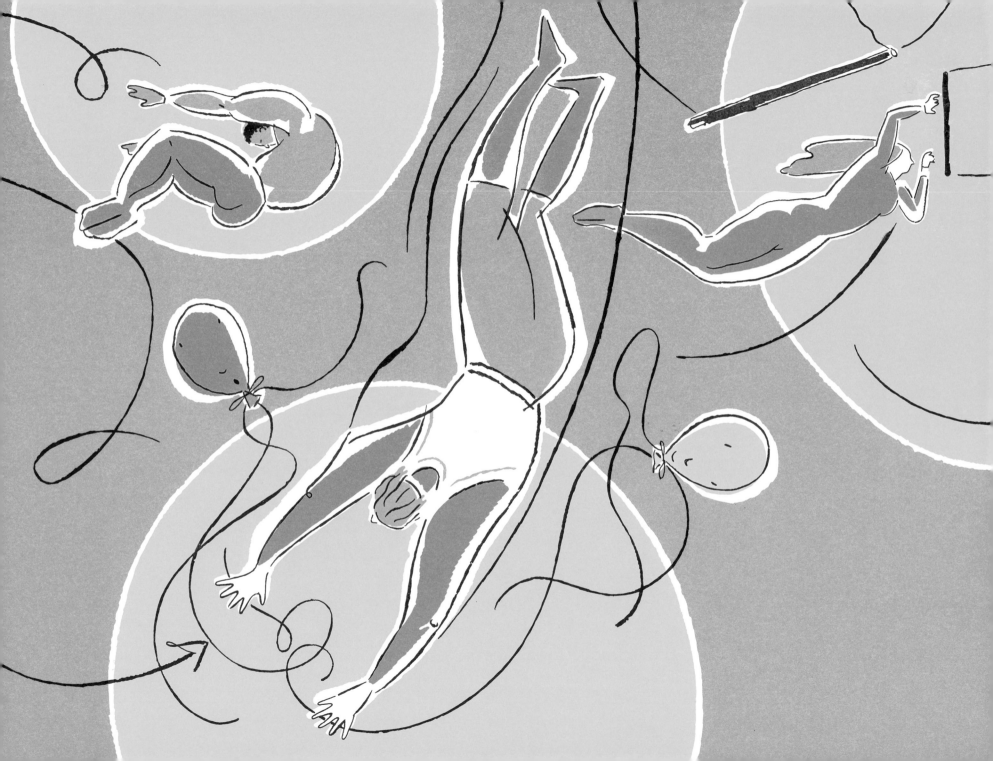

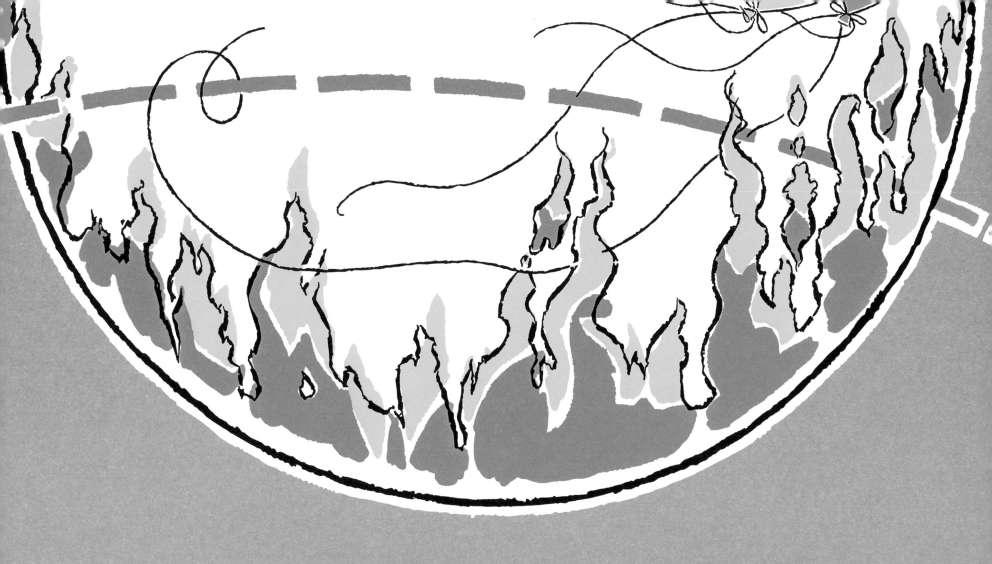

And the lions—
Well, maybe we'd better stay away from them.

...and give the dogs something to jump over!

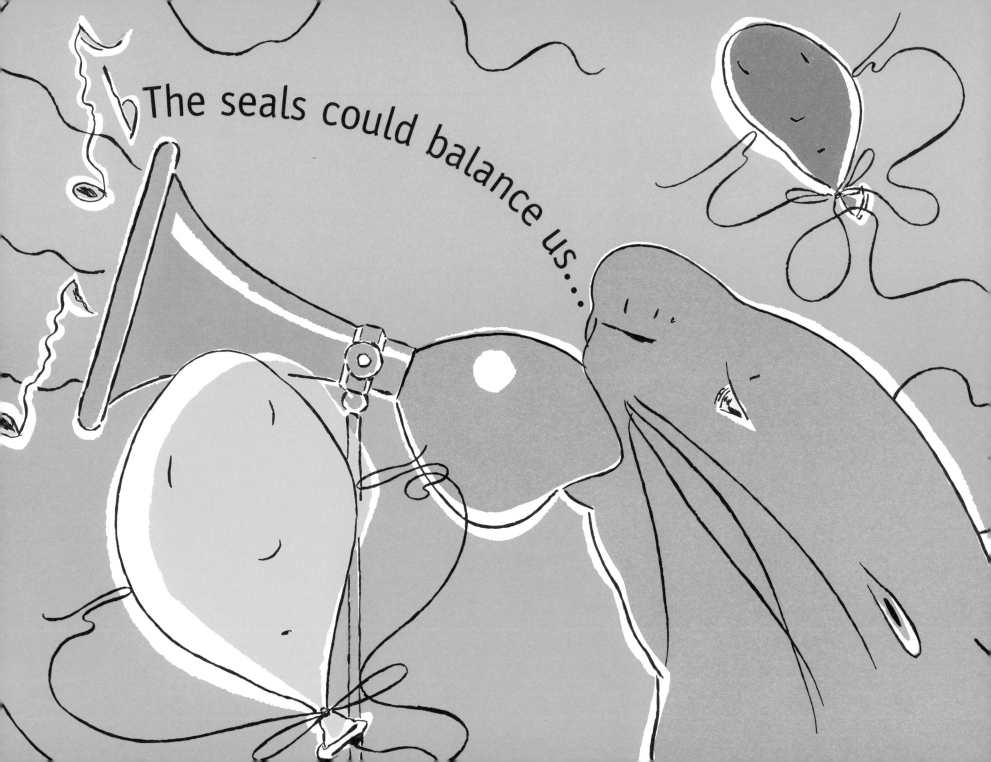

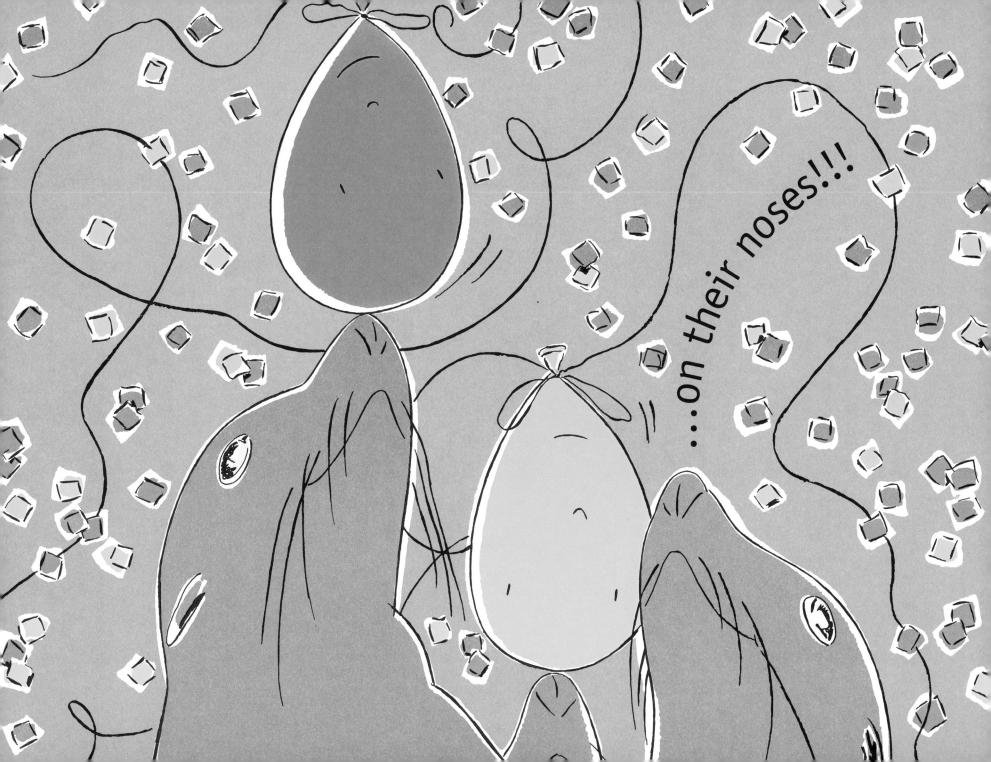

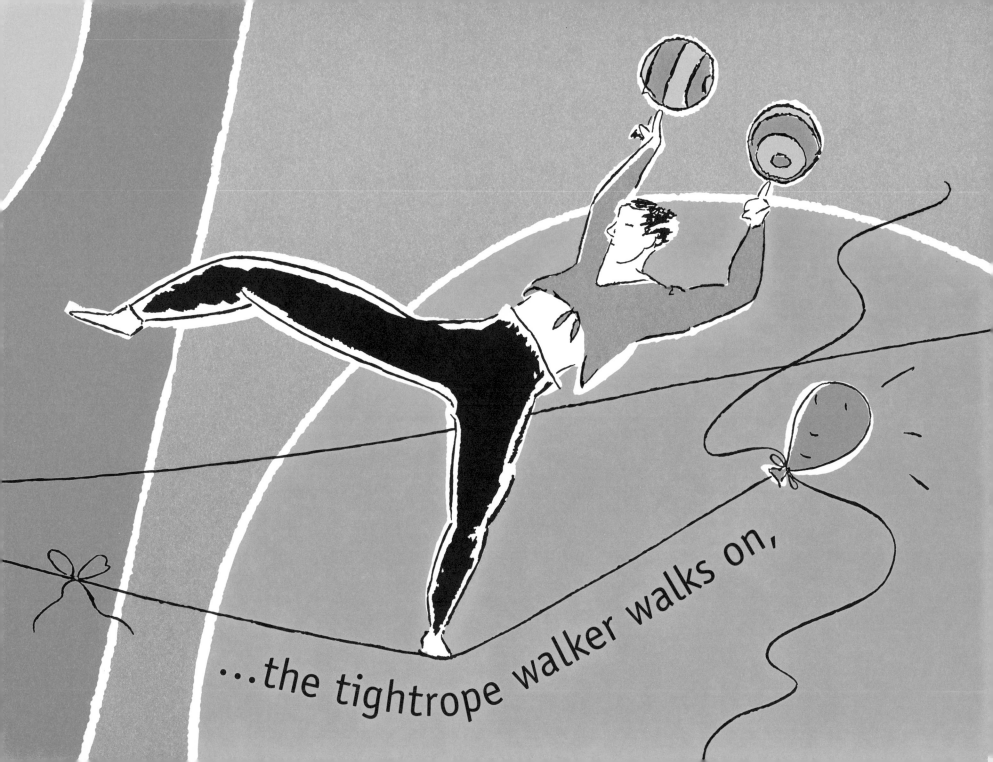

...the tightrope walker walks on,

And we could really help the strong man!

OOOF!

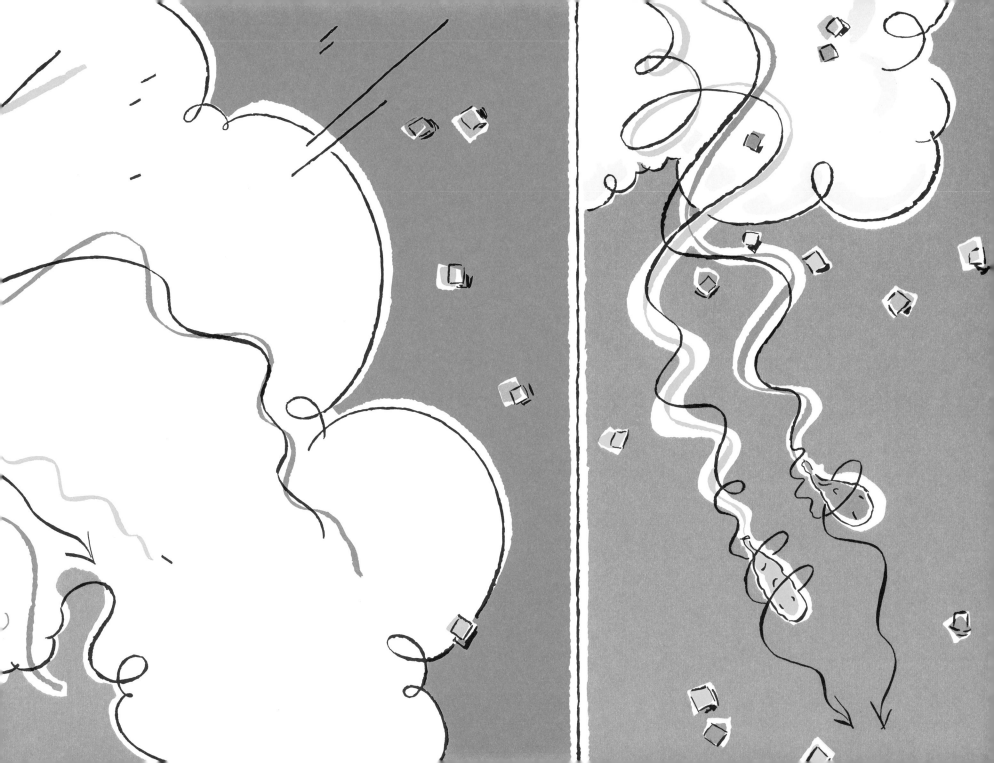

PLOP!

Sing a song of circus:
The circus has left town
And with it went the elephants,
The lions, and the clowns;
The trapeze star, the hairy ape,
The seals—the kangaroo!
But when it comes around next year—
We'll be there . . .

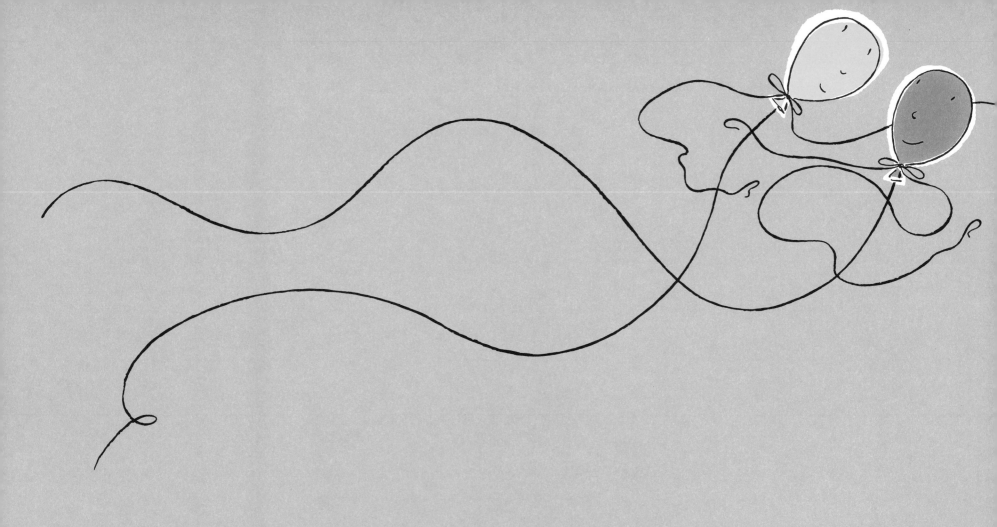

Won't you?

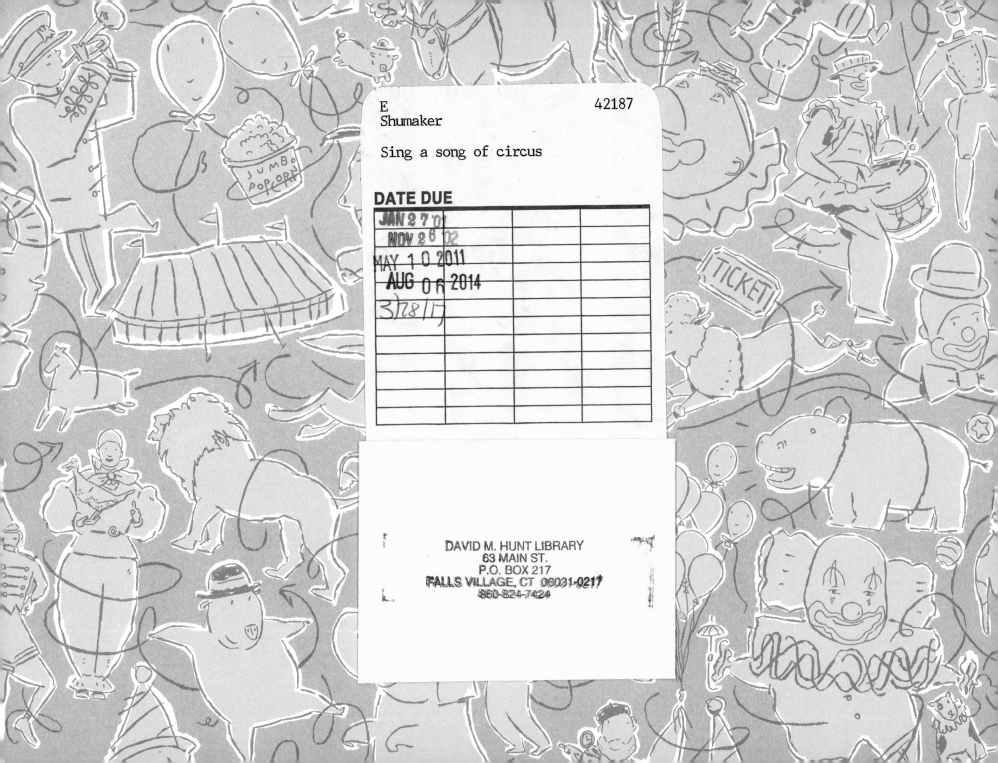

E
Shumaker

Sing a song of circus

42187

DATE DUE

JAN 27 01		
NOV 26 02		
MAY 1 0 2011		
AUG 0 6 2014		
3/28/17		